For Anna Grime, who does love a good shoe.
- Jackie Morris

For all who love.
- Ehsan Abdollahi

For thousands of years, people have been telling stories. From this rich global heritage, we can find stories that are strikingly similar but also different. *One Story, Many Voices* explores well-known stories from all over the world.

For teacher resources and more information, visit www.tinyowl.co.uk.

#OneStoryManyVoices #SecretoftheTatteredShoes

The Secret of the Tattered Shoes

Jackie Morris
Ehsan Abdollahi

TINY OWL

A soldier, weary from war, wandered
the land. His heart was heavy,
troubled by all that he had seen
and much that he had done, in
the name of the king.

In a forest, rich with the green light of
sunlight through emerald leaves, he met a
woman. He was a hollow shadow of a man.
She brimmed with light and life.

"*I am weary,*" he said,
"*tired of life. I have no wish to live.*"

Around them birds sang, an orchestra
of birdsong. He could not hear, ears
deafened by guns, by war.

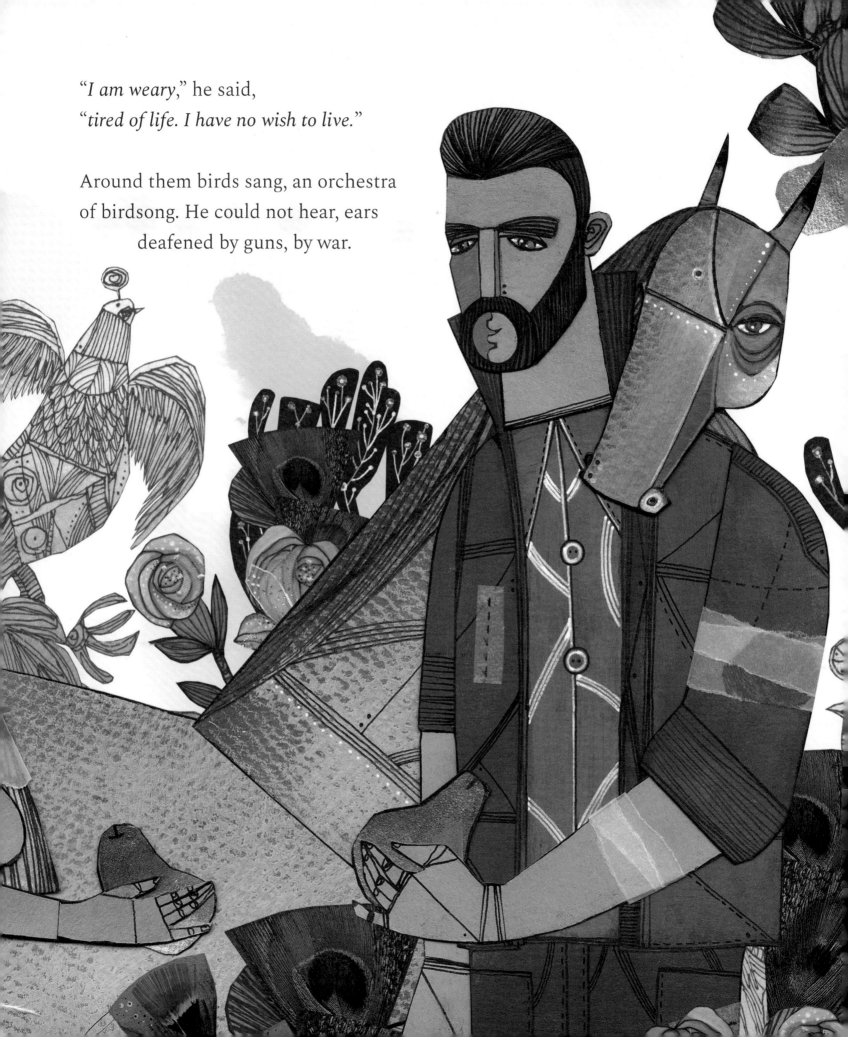

The woman took his hand for a moment. It was warm.

And she told him about the castle, close by.

"*The king,*" she said, "*has twelve beautiful daughters. Each night they go to bed, locked in a room with twelve great beds. Each morning they wake so weary they can hardly stand. Beneath each bed their shoes lie, each worn through, ragged and tattered. The king wishes to know why.*"

"*What has this to do with me?*" the soldier asked.

"*The king has declared that whoever finds the secret of the worn shoes can choose a bride from among his twelve daughters and rule the land. Many have tried. All have failed. Failure is punished by death.*"

"*Death is what I seek*," said the soldier.
The forest woman was sad. The soldier was
young and strong and handsome.

"*Go then*," she said, and showed him the path
to the castle. "*But do not eat or drink anything
offered to you by the princesses, and take this.*"

She handed him a cloak, mysterious as twilight, dusky like shadows, light as silk. *"When you wear it you will become invisible."*

The soldier took the advice, took the gift, and walked away. The woman and all the wild woodland creatures stood and watched him go. On her lips a quiet smile, in her heart a hope.

At the castle the soldier found a warm welcome.
A desperate king embraced him like a long lost son.
So many young men had tried,
so many now lay dead.

There was a feast.
He met the twelve.
They were all beautiful.

The soldier was shown to their chamber. Twelve beds with
rich covers. He was led to an antechamber, then the door to
the two rooms was locked.

For a while he could hear the princesses talking, laughing, as
they settled to sleep. The youngest came to him with a cup of
wine and a smile like frost on glass.

"*My sisters would like you to have this,*" she said.

He took the cup and pretended to take a deep drink from it, then lay down and closed his weary eyes. And he listened.

Owl hoot.
Far away, a wolf howl.

The castle settled
to sleep.

The princesses gathered around the sleeping soldier. The youngest reached out to touch his face.

"*Such a pity,*" she said.
"*So handsome.*
And soon he will be dead."
Then they ran back to their bedroom laughing softly.

Stone scraping on stone. The soldier rose, wrapped the shadow cloak tight around him, and followed the sound. Where a bed had been, now there was a stairwell, spiraling down.

Tap tap. He could hear shoes, stepping down the stones. Down, down, into the dark, twisting and winding, he followed. Each girl held a lantern.

Faster they went and he ran to catch up, stepping on the
hem of the youngest girl's dress. She cried out,
"We are followed!"
Her sisters laughed at her fears.
*"He will sleep for hours after
the drink that we gave him."*

The soldier followed, out from the twisting tunnel of steps to an avenue of trees lit by curious starlight. The leaves shone with silver as if painted by moonlight and he saw the girls wore rich dresses, as if for dancing.

He reached out a hand from beneath the cloak and *snap*, broke off a twig, and put it into his pocket.

For a moment, the youngest stopped, listened. He held his breath, waiting.

"*Come on*," called the others, "*they will be waiting.*"

On they ran, into the strange subterranean night, through an avenue of golden-leaved trees. Wrapped in the cloak the soldier followed.

Again he snapped off a twig. The gold leaves were heavy in his hand.

Again the youngest stopped. She thought of the soldier, sleeping. She peered back into the darkness behind, then turned and ran on.

Through an avenue of diamond-leaved trees they
moved and it seemed to the soldier that all the stars
in heaven had fallen to earth to hang in the trees.

He took the smallest twig.
It seemed a sin to damage such beauty.

Then they came to a lake.
Twelve boats, beside each
a man, tall, handsome.

The twelve princesses each climbed
into a boat. The soldier stepped swiftly
into the boat with the youngest, just as
it slipped from the strange shore.

As he rowed across, the man felt
the boat to be unusually heavy.
They lagged just a little behind.
But he had eyes only for the girl
and so did not see the dark
shadow of the soldier.

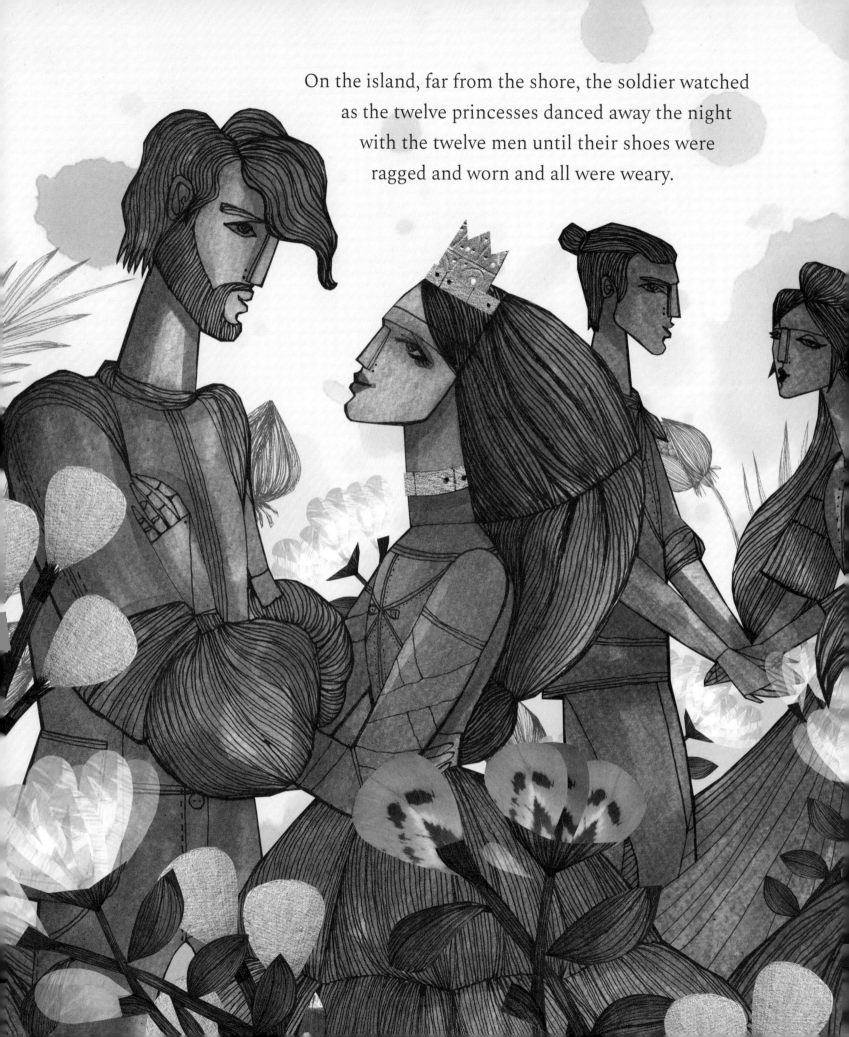

On the island, far from the shore, the soldier watched
as the twelve princesses danced away the night
with the twelve men until their shoes were
ragged and worn and all were weary.

He thought he had never seen such beauty.
As he wrapped the shadow cloak tighter around him in the
lights of the ballroom he remembered the woman in the
forest and thanked her again for this gift.

Just before twilight dawned each man led
his princess back to the boats, across
the lake to the shore where they
kissed. Then the princesses ran,
in their tag-tattered dance-
battered shoes, through each
of the avenues and up the
stone steps into their room.

Each tucked the worn shoes beneath each bed. The soldier had run ahead so when they peered into the antechamber the girls saw that he still slept and they smiled their cold smiles. He would pay for their night's dancing with his life, just like all the others had.

For the next two nights, the soldier followed the girls down the stone steps, through the avenues, across the lake to the ballroom.

He saw how they loved to dance, how each looked at the man with whom they danced, with such love in their eyes. He saw how the men looked at each of the girls as they rowed them across the lake, how they watched them go on their worn shoes.

On the final evening, he took a small goblet from the enchanted ballroom and hid it in his pocket.

On the morning after the third night, the king summoned the soldier before the court. He looked at the soldier. "*Do you have an answer to this riddle?*"

The soldier said nothing, but took from his pockets, one by one, a twig with leaves of silver, a twig with leaves of heavy gold, a twig that seemed to glow like stardust, and a small goblet of gold.

He handed each to the king and the girls looked on in horror. They knew their secret had been discovered. "*I will leave your daughters to explain*," he said.

The girls told their father everything and the king turned to the quiet soldier. "*My kingdom is yours*," he said. "*Which of my girls will you take as a wife?*"

The soldier looked at the girls, then turned to the king.

"I have been a soldier. I have fought battles for kings until I was weary of life and sought only death. When I watched your daughters dance in the enchanted ballroom, so beautiful, it warmed my heart to see such love. But how that love was won, and at what a price, made my heart sore."

"*So many died that they might keep their secret. And so, I say, I have had enough of kings and princesses. I met a woman in the forest. She seemed wise and filled with light and life. She was generous to a weary stranger. I will go and see if I can find her and see if she will dance with me.*"

And he turned and walked, away from the king and his kingdom, away from the twelve dancing princesses, away from the castle and into a new life.